Spaceboy Plays
Hide and Seek

Story by Michèle Dufresne
Illustrations by Tatjana Mai-Wyss

PIONEER VALLEY EDUCATIONAL PRESS, INC.

"Let's play hide and seek," said Spaceboy.

"OK," said the spacekids.

"I will be it," said Spaceboy.
"One, two, three ..."

The spacekids ran to hide.
Spacedog ran to hide, too.

"Look!" said Spaceboy.
"I can see you!"

"Look!" said Spaceboy.
"I can see you!"

"Look!" said Spaceboy.
"I can see you!
Here you are!"

"Where is Spacedog?"
said Spaceboy.
Spaceboy looked for Spacedog.
He looked and looked.

"Spacedog, where are you?"
said Spaceboy.

"Oh, look!" said Spaceboy.
"Here is Spacedog!"